What Do Cows Dream About?

written by **Kelsey Bonham & Shelley Sleeper**   Illustrated by **Shane Burke**

Dedicated to Grant, Gavin, Jackson, and Kendall.
Thanks for inspiring me. I love you.
-KB

Dedicated to my Mom and Dad who continually
encourage me to follow my dreams.
-SS

Dedicated to Koral, Kali, and Kamryn.
-SB

Happy Everything LLC

Copyright © 2013 by Shelley Sleeper & Kelsey Bonham
First Edition-July 2013

ISBN 978-0-9853621-8-8

shelleysleeper.com

Graphic Design by Francisco Macias O

Published by Happy Everything LLC

Printed by Sunrise Design & Printing Co.

18 17 16 15 14 13   10 9 8 7 6 5 4 3 2 1

Cows might dream about…

giving horseback rides.

jazzing up boring hay with some tangy ketchup.

Cows might dream about...

getting a field of kids to yell "HELLO!"

Cows might dream about…

going for a dip on a hot summer day.

Cows might dream about...

11

sleeping under the stars
in a big, comfy bed.

Cows might dream about...

guzzling chocolate milk through a loopy straw.

Cows might dream about...

15

bundling up on a cold winter day.

Cows might dream about...

getting down and groovin' to the music!

spending the afternoon trying to touch the sky.

Cows might dream about…

being an astronaut.

But most likely, they dream about…

a fly-free life!

25

FUN FACTS ABOUT COWS

- A young female cow is called a heifer.

- It is believed that the first cow arrived in the United States in 1611.

- Nearly every American family had their own cow until the 1850's.

- Gail Borden invented the condensed milk process in 1853.

- Louis Pasteur invented pasteurization in 1863. Pasteurization is the process of heating a beverage or food product to a specific temperature for a specific period of time. This process kills harmful bacteria that could cause spoilage or disease.

- Over 95% of all dairy farms are owned and operated by family farms.

- A cow must first have a calf in order to produce milk.

- Depending on the breed of cow they can produce between 5 and 25 gallons of milk per day.

- Cows have 4 digestive compartments.

- Every day cows eat about 40 pounds of food and drink almost a bathtub full of water!

- Cud is partially digested plant material that is regurgitated and chewed on again.

- Cows chew on their cud for up to 8 hours each day.

- There are 6 breeds of U.S. dairy cattle: Holstein-Friesian, Jersey, Brown Swiss, Guernsey, Ayrshire, and Milking Shorthorn.